For Sierra and Kira. Make a wish and follow your heart.
—T. M.

For Braydon, Mason, Landon, and my dearest Maddie.
I can't wait to see how far you will all go.
—G. L.

Designed by Megan Youngquist

Disney

How Far You'll Go

By Tim McCanna

Illustrated by Grace Lee

DISNEY PRESS

Los Angeles • New York

You're on a new
adventure!
It's challenging and fun.

You've come so far already,
but you've only just begun.

A journey sheds a
shining light
on who you are inside.

To reach your destination, let your

conscience

be your guide.

You'll likely face some choices,
and the answers won't be clear.
You'll search
until the right solutions

suddenly appear.

Down every path, you'll **overcome** a problem or mistake.

It's good to stop and

celebrate

the **progress** that you make.

To set out on
your **voyage**,
you will need some faith and trust.
Then add a little
magic,

with a pinch
of **pixie dust**.

You'll soon achieve
amazing things
for everyone to see—creating
possibilities
you never thought
could be!

Although you're good

and **ready**

to dash from **day to day,**

you'll find that

slow and **steady**

is a **wise and worthy** way.

But now and then
you'll **speed** along
as time goes racing by!

Your road is filled with twists and turns,

so keep a **watchful eye**.

In everything you strive for,
you'll add a special flair.
Each step will move you
forward,
and you'll know you're
almost there.

You have
abundant courage
to do what must be done.

You'll tackle any troubles,
and you'll **solve them** one by one.

But when you're feeling worried,

and your future is unknown,

take comfort that you'll never be

forgotten

or alone.

No matter how you build your home,

you'll stand with

strength and pride.

Your loving friends and family

are always **by your side**.

Prepare for years of practicing before your **dreams** come true.

The most important factor is that *you* **believe** in you.

Remember, when that moment
comes for you to
hit the stage,
your life is like a storybook,
and you can write each page.

You only have to
be yourself
and do your **very best**.

The world is waiting patiently
as you begin your quest.

You're bound for great discoveries.
Each day you'll **learn and grow**.
Now raise your sail and catch the wind.
Who knows

how far you'll go!